OLD FOOD

Ed Atkins is a British artist based in Copenhagen. In recent years he has presented solo shows at Kunsthaus Bregenz, Martin-Gropius-Bau in Berlin, Castello di Rivoli in Turin, the Stedelijk Museum in Amsterdam, and Serpentine Gallery in London, among others. His artwork is the subject of several monographs, and his writing has appeared in *October*, *Texte zur Kunst*, *frieze*, *The White Review*, *Hi Zero* and *EROS Journal*. *A Primer for Cadavers*, his first collection, was published by Fitzcarraldo Editions in 2016.

'Violent, emetic, immoderate, improper, impure – that's to say it's the real thing. Atkins' prose, which may not be prose, adheres to Aragon's maxim "Don't think – write."'
— Jonathan Meades

'Ed Atkins is the artist of ugly feelings – gruesome and smeared and depleted. But everything he does in his videos or paintings, I've always thought, he really does as a writer. He uses language as a system where everything gets reprocessed and misshapen – a unique and constant mislaying of tone that's as dizzying as it's exhilarating.'
— Adam Thirlwell, author of *Lurid & Cute*

'The universe is a rabble of contagion and miasma. The universe is a rabble of spheres, moved by mystical forces. Ed Atkins pokes this condition. He strokes and bursts it. He is the barber who doubles as doctor and a dentist, quick with his knife and flushes of blood. No page of *Old Food* is dry, it seeps with life, it breathes, bleeds, engorges, sticks you together with spit. Like bacterial cells on an errant loaf, *Old Food* is language in growth. '
— Helen Marten, 2016 Turner Prize winner

'Whether *Old Food* is poetry, dystopian fiction, script for an exhibition, metabolic literature or all and other, is up for discussion. What is not is the artist-writer's limpid poetics, carnal and hungry as the wolf. Atkins's writing is real and a relief. And if grammar is politics by other means, per Haraway, then so is food – as trope, as lack, as romp, as sustenance.'
— Quinn Latimer, author of *Like a Woman*

'Like a McDonald's hamburger or a cockroach or the Global Seed Vault, *Old Food* perseveres beyond mortal reason and enters a Beckettian afterwards. We cannot know the reason for all those tears, and it scarcely matters.'
— Vivian Rycroft

'*Old Food* will eat you up. Ed the head plays a vampire chorus singing of rotten old England, a magic wasteland which comes stuffed with a *Supermarket Sweep* of sinister flesh, goo, and other putrid treats. What's that growing in the kitchen sink? Stick the kettle on, love, and feel the sickness descend.'
— Charlie Fox, author of *This Young Monster*

'T.S. Eliot's definition of English culture ran right down to 'boiled cabbage cut into sections'. Ed Atkins scrapes in Cathedral City, battered calamari, excess margarine, peach cobbler, robin heart, Wotsits, mum, dad – and puts it all on a rotary spit of enjambing sentences. His turns of phrase are exceedingly toothsome: 'buttered, asteroidal crumpets', 'the lush, truffled / belch of Superunleaded', 'a crush of / neighbours jostling for gratis / crackling'. A post-apocalypse filmed on location in the colon of this country, every moreish page of *Old Food* is disgusting as a gastropub, the mince of a language going richly off.'
— Jeremy Noel-Tod, editor of *The Penguin Book of the Prose Poem*

'Reading like the accelerated brain patterns of a ravenous soothsayer-cum-scavenger-cum-time-travelling-salesperson, auto-translated into an almost recognizable diction, *Old Food* tastes of sick period drama, nostalgic for a time just around the corner. As singular as electrocution, it emits from the demented ditches, the euphoric crusts, disappointed hearts and bad gut-feelings as much as the patterned constellations, throbbing with multidimensional love-songs. From inside these erotic and squalid operatics, Ed Atkins revamps the scene of our selves. His writing advances like a daredevil knife-thrower, nervy and elastic, spinning words at the reader's throat.'
— Heather Phillipson, author of *Whip-hot & Grippy*

'If "Chocolate coins seemed doubly cryptic with the collapse of banks..." as Ed Atkins writes towards the end of this almost unbearable but compelling work, then dystopia and climate catastrophe are in our mouths and bodies: they pour through cataracts of names of herbs and meats and slime, of commonplace gestures in strange locations, they disrupt spelling and produce unnatural words and the suspension of proper grammar. Atkins' fiercely flowing anti-poetry takes up the disruption of unthinking indulgence at a point near to where Theodor Adorno left off, moralia now definitively below the minima we need to carry on – other than in the turbulence of the text.'
— Adrian Rifkin, author of *Communards*

Praise for *A Primer for Cadavers*

'Atkins emerged over a few pages as perhaps the most imaginative, sincere, and horribly, gloriously intent contemporary writer – certainly from Britain – I've read.'
— Sam Riviere, *Poetry London*

'Discomfited by being a seer as much as an elective mute, Ed Atkins, with his mind on our crotch, careens between plainsong and unrequited romantic muttering. Alert to galactic signals from some unfathomable pre-human history, vexed by a potentially inhuman future, all the while tracking our desperate right now, he do masculinity in different voices – and everything in the vicinity shimmers, ominously.'
— Bruce Hainley, author of *Under the Sign of [sic]*

'How can cadavers seem so alive, speak so eloquently? Atkins' prose is urgent, sometimes even breathless, seeming to stumble over its own material conditions. His is a unique voice that captures a truly embodied intelligence.'
— David Joselit, author of *After Art*

Fitzcarraldo Editions

OLD FOOD

ED ATKINS

'Affirming that the universe resembles nothing and is only formless amounts to saying that the universe is something like a spider or spit.'
— Georges Bataille

'My dreams have withered and died.'
— Richard and Linda Thompson

For Sally-Ginger & Hollis Pinky

OLD FOOD

Do it
at yourself an possession. Furtive seeking
empathic commons inside of a weak
charismatic dunce.

PERFORMER

Spring finds medium son just on the
floor. Looks maybe six? evil, holds
the red plastic-handled table knife in
a small right fist, fishes a slice from
the open bag of bad bread with a left.

Crumb-stuck margarine blouses
with the draw of the knife's few
dull serrations. Excess margarine
skimmed against the rim of the tub.
Margarine also stuck in a different
manner to the underside of the blue
foil peel, also. There is no margarine
at all on the lid of the tub that rests
against one um grey sock, looking
perfect, plastic, the lid. Margarine

also dark marls grey sock. Grey
sock's cuff's elastic
unambiguously resigned, wilting
round the blub edge of a pair of nice
slippers. Untucked beige polyester
short-sleeve also with margarine fat
seep tabbing, also. Lax brown cords'
shot waistband frayed low. Slight
merry muffin-top mini debouch? An
ease of flesh into the room.

Lighting is palpably dawning. Motes
and amber digits depend on young
blue air. All the visible skin would
shone with marge fat and the floor is
a ghastly rink with it in the corner a
whole family, their horse and worse.

*

What's at stake with the sandwich?,
to a crush of neighbours jostling for
gratis crackling.

Allegories used to be clear and
dogmatic as baby's beer. Foaming
teats sopped in The People's bra.

Later, eating just stopped. Snails
caulked black treacle, then. Then
wigged cassoulet and an humming
hard cheese wheel spoke thermal
death-time. Sorry year's Harvest
Festival focussed a depleted
congregation's prosy
grace of canned misc. and dry goods
for an lull for

example we'd prayer pack and tape
small boxes of unknown pulses,
Birds powder, powdered eggs,
UHT, mulligatawny cans for maybe
orphans who'd we'd prayed about
inside of their distant orphan fast,
woolgathering, we'd pray our blind
frippery as a romance of sorts an
unrequited cursorial, even as we too
had nothing to eat even at all. Was the
last of it, frittered.

In March we'd spoon molten
bootblack over its head and beat the
poor collie with an idea of tuck and
fuck and a steel ladle. Later we'd see

um them in the distance on a podium
speaking with candour, really very
moving. In winter we'd dress as low
ranking public servants we'd leverage
our status to hawk greengages and
whiskered courgettes and the twee
pickney gooseberries smote all
pressed on humid slices of
Soreen
with mustered portent and really cool
local slurs at a stall near the main
prison or thereabouts. Our banner
read 'Old Food' and could be read um
from solitary. Out loud we also had a
big bell we'd've rang.

We used to cut most everything
with fridge-cold clammy chicken
breast. Jelly or humour clot the grey
crevices and with the red dotting.
Red spider mites paused there, druft
down through the gone skylight
with other and more real bits of the
summer, seasoning a generous spread
of pokey galantines, upset duck and
I think quail. Charged with waves of

mortadella, fagged little Portuguese
chicken livers, garlic mosaics. Sieved
with unplanned soupçon willow
divers. We used to cut this with
cooling buttered chicken breast and
round lettuce secreting trace dry soil
in leathery green crinoline, served
demoralised with stooped blue cheese
dressing & hashed anchovies the
mouthfeel ringer for Dad's rank
eyebrows. Demoralised
like your dad was demoralised.

'A' was for Lowdown Horse, stabled
with a clutter of big black spiders that
were dead & crisped like sincerely
the nice tempura battered bangles
of calamari – only cold and sort
of a German forest. Solemn black
pubic do. Turning milk with weak
plums seep mar purple. Big black
spiders rattling about under the
horse, jostling sick and beards. Each
spider roughly the size and texture
of a sun-dried Scottie dog, wildly
dead. We'd lean over the paling and

count the ribs, gnawing grissini and
it never occurred to any of us. Then,
in the winter, out back eyeballing fog,
we might've be found gouging hot
buttered wool out the foiled bonfire
potatoes. Also, force-fed burnt
autumn sweep, also. Up the nose, if
memory serves. Piping bags of tepid
Smash expressed up lovely women's
noses in the poor, peccant gap under
the main prison right in the middle of
town. Like the main post office only
it was the main prison. And in the
barn, in the slack cow's crib, we'd find
hoary old cavolo nero burgeon and
we'd rip the bugger out and we'd cut
it with pale, clammy chicken breast as
well as with the shrugged-off brown
hen kip. It was condemned when we'd
got it.

We'd take care to thank people
for sending condolences and aid
in wintertime. It meant a um lot. I
mean I know it meant a lot to mum,
bedded down in the cold-frame or on

the roundabout with sweet william,
meadow mix, Nibbles. Oodles of
dropsical maggots and lice. The
maggots moving fast like junior
sea penises. They got all up in her
mouth and in her ears so that for the
longest time she could only declaim
in Martian, hear distant wars and/
or futures. Wiping tough tits, is
what. We'd've emptied a few sachets
of sherbet in there in her head and
chased it with a bottle of R Whites
then we'd smash mum about a bit till
she made some fucking sense.

Thanks for cleaning me up, Hannah.
We sent word of Hannah too, open
tool. We would send word of Hannah,
open tool.

Storied menace over beetroot-cured
salmon what poached in court
bouillon a mid-swim 'S'. Bouquets of
testy watercress fished out the ha-ha
at the bottom of the garden. Dandled
tarragon and apple mint, hustled at

the back door where drunks'd drain
their lizards and we'd stang furtive
lessons in dick grime and double
denim, snickering or draining it
under an busted golf umbrella stuck
in the balding turf. We'd cut the very
filthy whole with such lush chicken
oysters on good days. Or we would
laughing introduce ourselves into
the tight gap between the shed and
the neighbour's Ronsealed fence
where robust elder switch catted
one another's bare-faced & scold.
We'd shit on the elder if we felt like
it fuck it we took no shit. Cut with
the brown and boneless. Spineless,
really, but we'd hold on to the buckets
for planters or potties. Lugged coffee
slosh from Starbucks jakes to your
bed. We'd empty slowly relaxing up-
cycled boneless buckets of impersonal
bathroom coffee on to your um bed
while you were out. There was grease
piebalded the surface of the coffee, we
saw. And then
after that we'd get in the magnolia

bathtub and the water'd be just
livid with rust and the drinks'd of
course be little livid vodka jellies
served in sharp-hemmed fluorescent
plastic jiggers on wilting paper
plates, floaters and little emerald
swords like drawn boiled sweets
skewered lime tapers and candied
personal. Clattering boiled sweets or
clattering sugared almonds, toothed
rhyme sweet bone. Sucked to cutter
to cut the chicken's loose beige
sheath with sincerely speed for my
sister & spice for the older one and
using the sucked to cutter and that
plastic, scotched chopping board in
a turmeric snot colour. Then we'd
grease one another up and coast over
like the darling seal pups we were
over to Hannah's for profound &
deep kissing, wounds to servitude
yes. Then we'd get splay Analize
or Destroyer. Like crushed roast
potatoes gritted with Maldon and
black pepper. Broad beans and peas
and sweet marjoram, sage, lavender,

costmary, mint, clary, sorrel, savory,
parsley, fennel, basil, borage, orach,
hyssop, some houseleeks. Spinach,
cabbages, cole, lettuce, gourds, beets,
vines, raspberries, gooseberries,
violets, gillyflowers, peonies um
dragonwort, lilies, and roses. Wines,
vinegars. Verjuice, grains, oils, nuts,
peas and beans. One whole pat of
unsalted slathered with a subpoena
for stealing food we simply needed
to live or didn't need to live without
the imperative to steal to feel the
order of living, determined. Though
impassioned arguments concerning
the
right to live used not to be listened
to by those people who'd might
have been able to make a difference
anyway.

On Saturdays delicate chamois
crêpes sprinkled with sugar, ret with
Jif, rolled and cut and then we'd et
it with our mouths that were not so
much like mouths anymore but rather

snatched from the clart mouths of
babes or man-made grotto or shooting
off about the crêpe's contents and then
we'd probably make another one and
then we'd eat that one and also on and
with a or this lunchtime mouth.

Thank you for just opening your legs
the goose wishbone and the gavage to
engorge to torture. On thick, doorstop
toast with mustard seeds and sweated
green onions, served with a squat
glass of a cool, pale Sauternes and
with Hannah. Like an person with
rickets like a thing about sea urchins
churned like table tennis balls sawn
on the roiling surf was all we had to
eat, stranded on a voiceless rock in
the Pacific. We survived off of stringy
gulls snatched from the wind and
siphoned turtle blood, tart and pissoir,
leached from a ropy artery we nicked
with a razor in the um upturned
crotch. And at night we'd make out
at night, in the moonlight. And all
the grume and the sticky feathers

and voided turtle shells looked really
great in the moonlight. I suppose we
had drank more blood, I suppose,
than was the recommended. Surely it
felt like a bit much at the time. We'd
spoon and get delirious pondering
Wotsits, say, or just the type of peanut
prep that someone ordered or a couple
scoops of velvety soft-serve cassis
sorbet perched in a tan, sugared
waffle cone, folded and set with dad
haunting the Seine. Dipped and rolled
and lost. Followed by more really
great kissing with

confectioner's lips. Hundreds and
thousands to subdivide our love.

Months' trudge dwelled on yellow
omelettes limpid with butter, cheese,
chive darting. Lamb's lettuce coated
with an outgoing vinaigrette, our way.

Sunday lour bottle of chardonnay
passed about under the rampant
wisteria. Distant kirk carillon

sounded in the inert & bone air that
summer. Cypress trees thick with
doves to bang and to pluck. Blue
hills purpled in the near distance
bluddered fire and flaxen over wheat
fields and booze yeast nips whiffed
sank preludial loaves yawned with
a loving mist we'd catch wind of
outside and surf to this warm pie
source. We'd strip tight bandaged
saucissons and then ram them
bartered with beggars and retreating
combatants, skewered discs of sausage
on bayonets while they frigged our
bits to a squelchy win-win. Miles
and miles and months of this. Hot
coals and tanned leather, flanks,
quivers, chafing chainmail, etc. We'd
weigh ponderous dugs for equivalent
precious bijou, on the road. We'd
settle on a price way before we'd
set about one another's ravenous,
dribbling Holies. Like rats at the
angel basin. Honest to um we'd've
plucked a pinched little rotter right
off the curved spine of the earth and

dry-shucked it cold and there and
then if we'd've had to. We'd've cut
it with brick dust and rennet, glass,
and pushed little blush pucks of it
to Sirs and Hoochies if we'd've had
to in order to stay alive in the way
we'd become accustomed. And all
the time these dead nettles proffered
love with weeping aphids swept their
ivory choke of eggs, a whiff of minor-
key in Baroque ghost. We'd grasp
real nettles and human's necks with
similar resolve we'd whizz them up
into likely dire gurgle to daub the
snaking queue of epic sots.
Just and
put it in to calm the boil. We'd bring
plenty of things like that back to the
boil, then. Toy keels of cicatelli'd mob
the surf and loose a scum. We were
reminded of the journey. Drained
outside over an open sewer in the
evening-time, thinking of something
else. Served with a high puttanesca
to the lines of trudging human rind,
barely there. People were going

hungry. We'd tarns of steaming
chowder flotsammed with sweetcorn,
white fish, smoked hateful something,
hashed parsley stalks. We'd serve
as many as we could served with
regular fries. Secondi of osso buco
stuck over with sprigs of rosemary
and diagrammatic sections of glowing
oxtail in spills of separating tomato
and juniper jus. Loofahs of cheap
dry bread to sop up all the goodly
red. For the people. For afters we'd
had organised an audience with some
birds and a silly man. Some
days we'd plainly loll with the bottle.
A thousand souls swooned
step it
and later, in concert, dreamed
of eating their way out an sewn whale
carcass.

We'd wake May slick with sweat and
I'd immediately put my fingers down
the red lane and make you shoot the
cat and you'd fist me and I'd shriek
really really loud and throw up also.

The Mist would roll on in and we
deckhands would swim for it. Usually
we'd drown.

July saw us bottling water from the
outside tap. Afterwards we'd open
the bottle and drink the water from
inside of it, after and over a period
of time depending on whim and if
we were thirsty. The bottle, I mean,
with it's Quillfeldt flip-top stopper
and blow-mould heraldic doodad
meant we could charge a lot at the
service station. Times round the fire
we'd pump mason jars to the brim
with dark, resinous beer, sunk and
with stark, persistent head to dip-coat
nappy upper lips and dad-frenzy the
scant brains we'd hade woozed with
woodsmoke and tipless Camels. We'd
sing close-harmony divorce or the
black keen, percussive tapping on the
armour, gamebirds cooling just on the
floor or something.
Since packed grub wi' wet hay all in a
grave.

A white-hot slip of ballistic coal and
a great pearl fume would rise up
like the devil's own boff. Spadework
cold soil into the grave, we'd entirely
inter the grub for slow cooking,
religious larva. And for soft grub
we'd do this burying thing? Packed
grub with wet hay in a hole a grave.
Seven or maybe eight hours later
we'd disinter your dad and the skin
on him would be burnt and inedible,
basically, but the bushed senior flesh
beneath was really quite alright with
a few teaspoons of Colman's and a
quart of fassbrause. A bed of boiled
fiddleheads, dill pickles, capers.

Rainy days we'd make unboxing
videos of HDRs that'd bounce off
corrugated roofs of barns in tuneless
peals into fallow fields meanwhile it
was raining. Old slack heifers looking
on wet and angry, we thought, as
2,200 calories forced themselves into
the mud, mostly. Mostly they were
insipid stews of barley, pirate herb,

beans and potatoes, mostly. Fig bars to loosen our bowels for shitting, I guess. Clammy little towelettes from glossy plastic purses to wipe the remnants of poo off of our anuses and the surrounding part after we'd taken shits somewhere hopefully appropriate to take turd.

Then we'd unfurl yoga pork and then a groundsheet. Then butterflied high-tog sleeping bags of adorable rain-steeped homeless men like gaped hot soft sub buttered with cow chips and a kind of human marinara. Then um oak-smoked a union jack parachuted in slow motion, from the sky from nowhere, caught on the last brown gasp, flayed biddy swaddling finite persons we'd done, crated in what we called Cysts.

Pimpernel, primrose and groundsel and slean-cut black peat sod smouldered blue vegetal brume from the midden, doffed aboard and hoed to half-remembered peaks the pub.

Later we'd cut parachute silk
with skate wings and secateured
corrugated sailfish dorsals. Ripe
avocado, furrowed soft wet green fat.
Children'd cherish one another, there.
Bonemeal paste past use-by, cursed
by stoked fatties in town so no-one
could've et it save Hannah with her
ha asbestos constitution. Then the
children'd circle refuse, and parrot
steaming kiss-feed one piping grim
morsel to another, all drained flavour
and heat in the vespers. Tonguing
minced mouth to mouth, sweet pep of
ketchup filthed kids' cupid lips.

Urine used to turn to a kind of ghoul's
blood after the tenth go, though it
would remain warm enough for an
keck a awful lot longer. Quenelled
French cuss wet oxen whickered
off lush dandelion chaplets got
blanched to birch the newcomers.
They'd just arrived and we'd invited
them round for dinner al fresco,
down pretty English garden things

with bunting bordered by cheering
persons handing out cornflake cakes
in ruched paper things, stiff flapjacks,
paper bowls of Utz. Then we'd bade
them laid down in a nice big tin tub
built for maybe spastic veal calves and
we'd pour scalding pork fat over them
till they drowned or melted! After a
month or so we'd cut fat set slabs with
an hot scythe and dole them up a cold
cut deck on to the common, right on
the long grass, sobbing and screaming
and collapsing, us, retching.
We used to cut it with a blackened
pygostyle at Hannah's. Grieving was
this.

Those days we'd flack the sandwich
every chance we got. Alton Brown
discharge and mistletoe back in the
day. Reuben with Branston. Club.
In wartime cold hedgerow crumbles
dusted cold slimed vine leaves
attempted reinvigorated with drizzled
scant honey substitute.

Pitchers of lemon squash or night-
soil liquorice bum water to rid flaccid
dolmades.

Those days we knew how to eat a
witch: with gloves on and in one go.
Other nights we'd torch a village
just to bake an apple. Wadded with
suet and cinnamon, grated nutmeg,
sherry-macerated sultanas from the
big jar and two plugs of spongy bread.
Were bratted screams lapped flames
that devoured progress and minors
alike while we strained to see results
in a baked apple.

Dear Hannah, Thank you for saying
your tremendous nothing and doing
nothing. Thank you so much for
absenting yourself entirely. Thank
you for raising not a finger to halt
the head-kicking. Me somehow still
clutching a shawarma.

Autumn afternoons we'd serve
buttered, asteroidal crumpets on

misting Denbyware as the curfew
kicked in and no more bananas or
fruits? Or there'd be a Denbyware
bowl of warm jam tarts swimming
in warmed-thru milk with a stoup of
warm magic wine from Jesus' warm
middle for the very soul. We'd bar
the door as the sun set and the village
tocsin sounded a warning because
a pack of cannibals hunted about
at night. One Tuesday night they
managed to force their way into the
neighbour's and snatch the grandad,
rushed him outside in his pyjamas
and thumbed his eyes in then ate
him and stood there looking in at the
windows till morning. We used to call
hummus something else and we never
even heard of taramasalata. We did
used to have Turkish delight.
We did drunkenness most Fridays,
barged at The Jays, the shots. Pullt
heads marshmallow rafted sorry
Boddington that Paul pulled.
Cool wet chips' limp bouquet Put in
mayo and kiss me.

Cool wet chips wult down spline
and kiss me, duck. Then we'd dart
round back and vibrate to a middling
gas mark suitable for awful sweet
potato wedges and teenagers. Babies
used to smell of brioche and ham,
warm torn and egged down the
front. Served worn cropped Breton
shirts or darts short-sleeved silks
and olive green bombers, over the
stable door. We used to really drink,
then. Got dronk. Then brawling
in the car park. Pinning haha and
choking ha Vauxhalls, ha hatch-
backed decking fucking laying out
boys with their melt motorbikes,
jet black. Logo'd white and red
leathers'd creak and fluorescent
pink Kawasaki fuel tanks straddled
by the powerfully built boys. They
tended to like their hotdogs basically
eczematous with burn. Alleviated
with a soft, spaffed zigzag of French's
with a little wet babe puff. The burnt
boys. Everyone's Cokes had to be
Zero rather than Diet Coke and the

barbecue we had was orange and was one of those gas-powered ones but you had to use a long special match on, or the pink lighting wand to light it once you had first turned the bigger grey knob to probably the max at first only then to turn it down to a useable mid after. It did not come with a built-in sparking mechanism. The pink lighting wand had a long steel flue that was blueing a bruise at the tip, an ergonomic hilt & handle in hot pink plastic and an oversize black plastic trigger. The hot pink plastic was oranged from frequent contact with hot barbecue metal and burger spiff. The oversize black plastic trigger was knobbled for a human's fingers to go between the knobbles and squeeze a click. Most often boys gangs were on hand, tho, and would have to hand Harley Zippos they'd all be able to finger-snap alight. And then there was it followed the lush truffled belch of super unleaded. And I remember very vividly the twice-cooled touch

of steel slick with super unleaded,
pried from a boy's jean's watch
pocket. Lovely blistered bell peppers
and gawping caged fish on the
bone till late. Broadcast flakes over
Hannah's tabouleh, which was tough
and cheap with parsley stalk, watery
cucumber die and also those watery
little tits of tomato, disappointed
unmoved, as if from Holland. A
large metal bowl of fiercely garlicked
yoghurt. Cultivating an red plastic
plate with the yoghurt, then planting
fast-cooling demispheres of pared and
roast beetroot to leach purple slur and
incriminate the fingers. Cold-pressed
Cypriot drooled gorgeous and opaque
shine also lemon juice and each of us
would track dips with lavash canoes.
Biker's greased. Turns out hummus
is really lovely, says one boy. Stocky
green bottles of ownbrand pils to
wash down squeaking erasers of hot
& salty halloumi. Come spring we'd
wrap it up and take off. They say the
stench came to define an era.

After winter's toil we'd drag our rigid
bones and heavy hearts to the hot
spring where we'd dip in unison with
a bloody sun and steep till the plaque-
like smegma solvent and a kind of
stock billowed in the moonlit water
cut with cock. Perched on the rocks in
white towel dressing gowns, sipping
thin chicken broth from rough grey
pottery, we looked really good and
really relaxed. Our raw callouses
thrummed deeply, softening, and
fatted lice loosed from our scalps
and pits and would drift dead to the
surface and jounce about like stoned
quince. Hannah'd make a kind of
faux frangipane tart while some
of us got off. Served with some ok
vanilla ice cream and one or two huge
powdery wafers from the shop. Rowed
out by a child in a tiny willow coracle,
singing the high dirge. Polished
off with a splendid liqueur made I
think from Mirabelle plums, and a
single mordant knob of Maroilles.
A couple more hours floating about

on our backs, gazing up at the sky
and talking in hushed tones. Soft and
gurgled poorly informed exchanges
in English. Meanwhile our tips got
pruned and we'd so often just shut up,
give up and kiss each other.

It used to get dark much later than it
does
now but altogether faster. Back home
via the field with those dead kids in it
just lying there and into the one bed.
Morning's thrusting while a weak
sun rose. Old horse's starveling face
comes in at the window like someone's
forgot grandad, ha, mooching for
whatevers. We'd fix some very
narrow grits and stir what was left
of last night's jugged hare thru and
plonk a wooden bowl of it on the
pavement and watch the horse near
heart-attack itself gobbling the mess.
Afterwards we gave it some more
and then a bit more and eventually it
looked a little calmer and more like a
horse. We'd sit opposite one another

and bail an gory jug with some walnut
bread, scheming. Webbed diagrams
drawn across the griddle in dropscone
batter, tasty scabbing and dotted
with mum's currants. Stacked on a
wicker something, the scones detailed
spells to fill holes, starved tummies.
Gnawed plastic cups of Ribena
made to Mark's strength while the
sun stayed put and a winged demon
passed across its face like a cutter in
black. Over there the horse screamed,
I think, and the hearth went out and
we drank our Ribenas and opened the
Cathedral City in silence. The soft
push of a small knife. Silent reseal,
glance, *Pause*.

All summer'd we'd um hung it, with
all of the natural enzymes to make it
age well but then suddenly we only
missed the window of opportunity
and loads of flies made it go bad with
their repeated ralphings and it near
liquefied off the hook. Even though
if it'd went brown and puddled latex

in trash we'd probably still've eaten
it for visions and the purging sweats
and to have had something to eat.

Wisdom, Mark said, was ever in an
apple, so warm calvados followed
bright suppers at the mansion on
occasion. Or sweet dewy rum baba,
dreggy Turkish coffee and cigarillos
at Easter. Salted caramel shards
golden crazy paving a platter of
hollow milk chocolate eggs containing
maybe a week's wages or otherwise
just a horrid gurk of Sir's, like
chitterlings and pickle or His Ham.

There used to be justice rather than
I don't know chocolate eggs. There
used to be rallying cries'd rather than
just a rich man suppressing belches at
you. There used to be an unopened
box and an open front door.

We'd feign fun at all this behaviour,
laughing along and wolfing the
choccy. Then, when he'd gotten

his machine out and sure dandled
a weepy staffer, we'd put him on
the fire and hold him there till he
entirely stopped. Then we'd live in
the mansion forever and do whatever
we wanted to do with it and what we
wanted to do at each other, living

off of the land and the broken backs of
newer serfs. We became happy brutes.

On the weekend we watched everyone
else thereabouts dance or maybe it
was a battle. We had snacks we had
ramekins of a rhubarb fool with
Plain Digestives crumbled on top!
We passed around a bag of malted
milk and vodka. The fool then got
skin on it and the milk spilled in the
dark while we watched it all unfold,
holding hands. Over the course of the
next week we trawled the surrounding
fields and woodlands and managed
a haul of maybe thirty, thirty-five
people. Peeling off their clothes and
sparing them, I suppose.

First, there was the elevation of
the barn laid out on the front lawn.
Whitewashed and with shiny black
faux-Tudor struts and some I don't
know daft sgraffito. Lacquered
with countless liquid tonnage black
crude chased with a massive curbing
silence. A chaser of silence to curb
the paralytic. We'd used to watch
loose Vs of geese off somewhere
sometimes, honking. Bleached device
on the billow, breaking up. The slow
wane of intelligibility. Light used
to travel quicker than sound so that
flying geese and their honk didn't
seem to be of one from down here,
even though they must have been
of one. Certainly, we never once
could ascertain which of this or
that goose in the scarce V sourced
what honk! The geese passed and
blether overhead. They did not see
nor did not recognise their clipped
kin terrorising the foul yard down
below, pitiable, hissing and sneering
and jabbing at puddled reflections.

Winter we rang their Haught &
Strang and did a part-exchange in the
pub. Some people were hungry but
had lots of wood. Hannah plucked
the one goose we'd kept it was maybe
a Sunday at this point. It must've
been a Sunday or a day made Sunday
by occasion. We studded it with
black cloves for eyes and slathered
it with Gale's runny honey. We
stuffed it with Paxo Sage & Onion
and some lemons, optimistically.
Garlic, uncertainly. We did not have
any potatoes or red wine. We ate in
silence after a ridiculous and familiar
argument. I bolted mine because
everyone else was being a dick and
not even eating theirs. Oesophagus
aching, I cleared everyone's plates
and scraped everything into the bin
and went to my room to cry and listen
to something sad and maybe phone
Mark. Downstairs apparently they
all cheered up enough to watch a film
all the way through. The next day we
concentrated on the family duck's one

egg and then it rotated slowly on the
spot and hatched an awful man we
then had to eat.

Solace got in hot, thick, boggy rarebit;
two or three glasses of a chilled
Beaujolais. Worse, burdock out of
stock. Saffron was astonishingly
cheap compared to nowadays. Oysters
was white sick. On the table we
had bowls of two types of heritage
tomatoes, red and a purple. Two
lukewarm croissants on a little olive-
wood board. A slightly recessed
enamel plate-bowl spilling over with
lemons and three cocktail limes.
Miniature hass avocados. Modest
flutes of cava. Finished coffee cups
and crumbed plates, remnant red
and purple smears. There was an
hourglass that counted, I think, a half
hour in black volcanic sand, I think.
Egg on brick. Guzzled beaker of
sweet white foam and returned mucus
striped with, I think, hen's blood?, I
think.

We'd make pasta from a manioc
flour, one basilisk egg and some
acid I remember bread and I found
it myself, tossed in a sap on the edge
of town at night. We dried it out
perched on the radiator and sawed it
up and pulled knifefuls of crunchy
peanut butter across the powdery
faces of that bread and while we ate
both peanut butter and reconstituted
white loaf stuck speech impediment
to the roofs of our mouths. Reciting
rote with lisping inverted lids of
chumbled peanut butter and white
bread, rawlpluggery & grout. We've
very vivid memories of late autumn
plucking tender meat from the meat
trees. And in short order cardboard
trugs brimmed with thick good
floor meat. Meat were driven from
the warren employing the honey-
coloured dachshund and shot meat
to a halt on its back. We bore arms.
A couple wet revolvers in gun-metal
grey. Three long wet rifles we'd
cart about in a barrel. Red nukes in

bespoke hods. We had had a square
meal the night before the campaign
begun. Tempura-scabbed zucchini
tutus stuffed with ricotta and spinach
followed by lamb's sweetbreads, black
butter. Capers' violent ellipses, too.
Sated, we'd wage war on parent-
teachers who'd kick us hard and
crumb us and serve us so scalded to
pristine siblings as seeming goodness
that didn't need a knife really, it
came away that easily. Plucking easy
meat off at range with a scope. Soft,
yielding meat at school and at church,
very easy plush abattoir. Oftentimes
served more easy sweetbreads
scooped with the melon baller from
done legbars that scored the fowl
yard in the summer. Skewered on
cedar picks meticulously fanned on
emerald majolica, walked about by
Granny trailed by Hannah carrying
a little blue plastic tub of dzadziki and
the contorted amphora with raki in.
The amphora had been made by an
ex-con and depicted all the murders

in black figure. The raki pearled
louche meltwater inside our glasses
just like the changing September sky.
Turnip juice jiggers for old bastards as
oestragenated blood omens and read,
like grounds, like omens. Granny
would told us it was all over for us
that we should break for the hills and
not look back and well we didn't heed
shit.

Granny predicted the PKQ ages and
ages ago as though

they weren't new. Once, she said, she
stopped A Arrow with her chest and
A Dog with a devastating song she
knew by heart and then Granny'd
savour-suck crisps to compressed
beige pap in her weird, happy mouth,
one by one, sluiced from cuss-
crimped tongue and pink bone lath
to scrotal gullet with sups taken of
piss-weak luke raki, taken slow with
her eyes closed and after everyone
else had certainly gone, attentive only

to the calm burblings in her head and
the muted memory of goners, lovers.
Her hands were polished with burns
and she could scarcely stand it.

She'd recall unfurling freshly baked
tuckshop Chelsea buns, skinned tan
with demerara and burnt currants
with dear friends. Yards of warm
moist cake and pretend drank
divvied up among some great friends
arranged aggressive and outwards
on a fallen birch in unnecessary
uniforms one long summer in a
private grove they scaled a chain
link fence to enter. Friendly sex in
the mornings under Seurat dappling
and some bath coffee with railway
cream. Scotched eggs with smacked
sage. Great blithe yolks with papyrus
whites. Polystyrene blocks of
Beyaz peynir bogged suggestive in
viridescent olive oil. Proud purple
kalamata nipples plus the black
polyps Crespo from a can after sex,
dredged with zaatar. Frozen pitta

disks heated and distended on the
tava then cut into soldiers and jostled
into an artful heap. We'd eat hot tapas
off of one another, then. Glazed dicks
docked anus, powdered sugar & hot
brown churros pussy. We'd luck our
clotted hands and titter, chasing about
the yard and scattering the legbars,
thrusting game groins for little stole
kisses and fingered, and unusual
wattles done simple and rousing in
a strawberry-blonde pakora batter
pepped with mirin, Sichuan pepper
and head.

We told a man about stiffies and fixed
the roadside whispers of workers jugs
of a wet caipirinha in a gorgeous July.
Turns out tramping makes people
hungry, so we swung a tray of happy
little beef sliders and a few sorry
onion rings to brought what looked
like smiles to their weather-thumped
faces. Hannah wept as she wrenched
and clawed at the tramps' necks.

We slept gross and happy at night
while mum gathered a nocturnal
yield of forced rhubarb in old palm
baskets that creaked in time with the
flush shoots' groan by candlelight.
We'd join cults, I think, in our sleep.
We would join death cults in our
sleep that had flamboyant leaders and
silver tureens spotlit in apses and the
charismatic leaders with daddy's face
would solemnly give out really quite
generous portions of delicious Cullen
skink or maybe caldo verde right into
our imploring faces and we should
be grateful for it. Malted drinks were
done with hemlock at bedtime and
we'd all keel over fun dead. Thank
heavens for the morning: Lambent
sun remedied the lurg and delivered
good flavoured yoghurt and a sterling
central Jenga of traditional golden
shortbread for play to get us to eat.
Some bath coffee and Hannah's
bleak recital with her remaining left
hand creeping from the other room.
We would convey the yoghurt from

ramekin to mouth using the bars
of golden shortbread. As in, we'd
scoop the rhubarb yoghurt from the
ramekin using the bars of shortbread
and no spoon. We didn't even know
what a spoon was spoons came much
later

then durn wooden airplane trays.
Heat-sealed insect protein with
kale hoick, balled hâche. Freeze-
dried ratbag shavings steeped in
cold nozzled android milk. Joltfish,
curved, driven smooth over pack
ice. Curled plastics hued pollen
in a permanent spaff. Pink plastic
cups of Commemorative Juice over
bloody pack ice. Hurled camomile
dog, wilted cooled, greeting. Drawn
jellies over pulled kid a monthly rite,
totally mash on Snakebite. And with
a wicked jollof in the giant hollowed-
out skulls we'd salvaged from the
clinker as with the spinach-riven soft
wrapped dead falafel mildly junked
with special tads of pickled red

cabbage plucked from the beautiful
and generous daddy's special votive
jar. Unclean headcheese with a whole
moon and an coughed bark of moth
talc. Witch's compress thumbed
pockets, grilled and lit loads in a
inverted witch hat made from black
theatrical muslin to strain a simple
paneer. Intricate folded filter distilled
basic gore into a concentrate to clean
all the shitty kecking off of the tent.
Rain would lash the tent incessantly
and months would pass in a fasting
torpor. Outside it rained and rained.
We saw the future, then and
one unforgettable wet Wednesday
we managed to pack the devil with a
holy relish, vim and beat and rinsed
subsequent turned orbs in a kind of
bleak float
basic viscera, fulsome and sustaining
a darkening part of history, then. We
changed permanently.

Christmastime! Little brown yule
bowls served at the end of the

procession, at the gates of St James'.
Pounding at the gates Deliver Us!
We'd sup, careful of the broken plate
glass, wary of the rusting hulk as
mistakable goddage, sour lovage;
parsley soup with a spiral of cream
and a hot ciabatta roll each. Pretty
fingers of baked salsify, bronzed
with a blowtorch and served as it
should be, with pink Himalayan
salt and a plastic flute of prosecco.
In the ensuing conflagration brown
bottles pooled and potato reliquaries
broiled and anything made of paper
or cloth or wood would got consumed
then cat ash flocked sheep's cheese.
Fires apostrophised the horizon at
night, legible from thirty thousand
feet. Fires blaze in crook greens
apparently because the crimes was so
awful.
Books could be like cakes or like
sandwiches. Fat books could not be
baked but they could actually be
slathered with demi sel and a mature
cheddar and full you up, uselessly.

Books would burn their way to ash
if you put them in a lit black oven,
especially if liberally wot with a stole
ancestral poteen and forgotten as what
they are and more thought of as a fuel
like absolutely everything else.

In June 2009 we made beans on
buttered toast with a copious strew
of grated cheddar on top! Sometimes
beans engulfed a hot buttered jacket
potato. The pooling butter and slower
pooling cheddar'd regularly fairly
clarify the beans' juice brim and
steam would fret our NHS spectacles
and full air with a mellow whole
loving, seducing slow droves of wasps
to coat the floor, coming right in
the door across the floor. Enervated
wasp rug genuflecting right at dinner.
Wasps were at their most dangerous
in the autumn, then, near-death
slouch heedless at a pear core on the
sill, perhaps, or um lunging at some
of Hannah's flat lemonade. In the
autumn, wasps were all spent and sad

and incurably. Hannah would lug empathy to the insects, even. Wasps didn't used to make honey but their teetering paper estates brought up wood gook were outright astonishing. Toy honeycombed church of weightless human sacra, pet ghost's sacrum, dreamt dried, stilling as burnt to death homes, Fridays.

One bleak hanger right on the edge was a hell signpost with jilted wasps' nests and also liquefying black hay bales, piled and picked out nights by a low blue. Nothing at all lived there except deposed Royals, high up on crude ply platforms, bundled against the cold in squirming, cack-striped ermine. Midnights we'd winch entire swans up into the rafters and run away and after a few minutes the Royals would emerge, unfold to their full shocking size and, overly naked, move slow across the vaulting, dislocate their jaws and basically yammer a swan inside of a

remarkable silence. We watched thru
the splits, noiseless and motionless we
didn't move a muscle. You didn't even
need to pluck the swan you could
just
pinion it with whatever wooden piling
to hand and lightly kneel on its neck
and put a little cut in its carotid then
quickly drown it in a big mazer of hot
spiced stout. We'd fish it out after an
hour or so and strap the shambles to
a pallet with bungee cords and drag it
out and down to the hanger.

Afterwards, in the basement, we put
away a gigantic ablutionary Wiener
schnitzel, served with a morass of
deteriorating potatoes from the big
white chest fridge, a crock of slow-
addling redcurrant jelly, some safe
Grünerveltliner. Hannah would
lead us in some rousing catches and
we'd more or less forget the whole
distress. The average metabolism of
a royal was about one-fifth the speed
of an person's. Royals' stomachs

contained there three compacted blue
letters to tackle the feathers and fur,
the bones and nails. Crack one of
their otoliths in half with a wooden
mallet and you'd could yes suss
berserk millennia, identical. In the
afternoons ghastly capital feedings
binged coronal sceptres and gold-
capped teeth till all the forests got
sacked and the shorelines stripped
for the monthly out-of-town patellas.
We were put in charge of dry-peeling
woodland animals or else deboning
a jumble of game-birds for the
spectacular New Portmanteau Meats.
Red robin heart inside an robin inside
a crow inside a tenderised small local
shark and a dog inside some brined
scat inside of a big black glossy bull
with its hips specially luxated by
vet to just get it all in there. Herded
into a capacious metal gulley in the
middle of makeshift arenas on the
outskirts of every market town. The
mob that gathered hollered ravenous
approval as the bulls – tottering taut

upholstered with dead up inside of,
vastly drugged – got pushed over
by computer design and engulfed
in a river of scalding red garlic
tot. A press of cute, terrified deer
slid down a lubed chute, down into
the join, followed by hundreds of
bound notched geese. Colts trussed
with their own untwined indigo
guts, flanks massaged to a sheen
with truffle oil and flocked with
truffle shavings um douched from a
computer-controlled hose from above
and then set alight and then snuffed
out with a hiss on forlorn contact
with the hot wet. A little later all of it
was stirred automatically with twin
pink silicone rubber paddles the size
of the roof at home. It sounded very
loud. After an expectant while the
crowded terraces had pneumatically
jolted forward into a bluff slant and all
the seating and railing and terracing
retracted into polished steel place
and everyone slid in as prepped veg,
helpless into the drink. Some days

later last limb thrashed out and the
agony finally ceased and, pause, then
a fanfare via loudspeakers and so
opening yucky elderly monarchical
family vent and out skad. Come
evening fragile children materialised
like static and et well.

Traditional Tuesday's robot-rinsed
durian salad, soused with warm
custard by the hearth, hearing the
croon, dragged outside for beg.
Nursing blue mugs of soupy brown
stiffened with a wee bevvy. Alcohol
used to be served to the elderly first,
till we realised the elderly were no
better than anyone and that history
and experience bore no necessary
correspondence with worth. An
given palate's susceptivity, however,
generally corresponded with the
quality of the alcohol served.
Meaning old assholes were content to
kill carafes of Blue Nun while
tucking in to more warm, khaki-
coloured pap. We'd get Pomerol.

Bristol Cream would kayo,
afterwards. Babies, too: a tad of
Plymouth pipetted on browned
rubber teat would clear flake to kip.

Late summer; dwindling light;
pristine white Irish linen hemmed
with drawn thread-work.

Hannah's silverware'd be set Parisian
style, with tines and bowl downed.
The bread knife lay on the knife-
rest next to the bread plate. A butter
dish with dentic lid, to hand. A
sherry glass. Mother of pearl caviar
spoon. Snail fork and snail tongs and
a cocktail fork. Alsace glass, soup
spoon, fish knife & fork were dorsal.
A black bone dish next to the charger.
Lobster pick, lobster cracker in the
shape of a lobster. A burgundy glass.
Entree fork and also knife. Ice cream
fork? Puling over a meat knife &
fork? Salad fork & salad knife. A
finger bowl and a champagne flute. A
cheese knife and a nut pick. A dessert

fork & a dessert spoon. Individual
crystal salt cellar with spoon and
sterling silver lidded crystal pepper
shaker. The candlestick holders
were pewter and the candles were of
mutton tallow that sputtered a cheap
fry-up when lit. We'd leave all this
out for a week or so then put it on the
floor very carefully.

Come summer, waste fed to the jolly
brown pigs. In winter we'd be very
hungry so we'd of course eat the pigs
which meant the following season
and forever afterward we didn't have
any pigs they were extinct we'd just
chuck everything we didn't finish in
a hole in the historic forest. It came
out, Hannah'd said, over an ocean
of fire. Our shit kept it burning, she
said, the earth turning, the seasons'
laggy wheel spirn. Desperate winters
we'd fling as much gash in there as
we could so as to hurry the arrival of
spring and the return of any finger
sensation at all.

Calm pools matte crackle rime for
ages in a pale blue found only when
next to a creeping sun's dawdling
reds, oranges. And the hounds' pack
thudder clouded their meaty huff,
furbishing little ovoid looking-glasses
in the frozen puddles, with spat fist
meaning foxed game or the Sirs'
limitless vanity. Held in their dog lips
like they were their own blind pups.

It was ever easier to simply remove
the breasts with an knife and ditch
the remainder, rather than commit to
the arduous plucking, but they'd take
your hand if the birds weren't wholly
bald and otherwise unscathed, tho,
so. An informal lunch of pot-roast
pheasant, swum over with loaded,
swarthy prunes and a plausible
Armagnac; dry mash, weak cabbage.
Sirs got racy in the dining room.
Urns of mulled wine kept wassailers
blasted and tuneless till red bowls
of bread pudding calmed with a
thin Dairylea weep, surrendered

sultanas and frangible moments of crystallised sugar roofing. We'd load long white clay pipes with thatches of a dark shag threaded with Mike's lenient hash dispensed from a panel of vinyl'd chipboard, cheap jigsawed heraldry, and a smouldering hemp cord, wearing flat, white, charmless masks made of I think hide. Ducked out through an open sash on the south side and sprinting out across the dewed lawn. We'd exit civility and re-enter the feral and humid and tidal-smoothed, crudded with red earth, blue woad, lucked toad backs and whole praffed adder peel, shrilling in a blackened pan of raw butter, sod fire puked acrid plumes attacked the bridge between the nasal bit and the throat. Then the smell of reptile beef and Hannah'd think of all the kitchens in the world and describe them in exquisite detail.

Fleurie? Drinking used to be as basic as upending an animal's open

neck into your mouth. We used to
open an animal and simply tip what
come slipping out into shot glasses,
drinking until nothing more came
out or what was coming out was cool
and grey and made you down, washed
away with a smaller animal's openup
or some oat milk.

Custard tarts hot from the oven were
welcomed by sundry cousins down
for the weekends of Augusts. They
were wiry, angry types in sacking
and had broken skin. They would
bring scarcely edible shite from their
homeland and recipes to follow writ
on curling velour in a language we
couldn't look at nor, then, follow.
Foreign muck that howled in the
pot, our cousins nodding, wounded
fled to be sent back for seconds,
gorgeous and us full of their dread,
their astonishing solids, fibrous rent
bum heat and panicked tongues to say
what?
Death?

Miracle

death? I didn't know.

September, news reached us of their
entire craven system just not. We'd
mourn them traditionally: without
a second thought. There was feasts
of filled bread, though. Bananas
weren't available. Burgers were quite
something, sat happy in a celeriac
remoulade. The webbed cream guts
of vast marrows would turn out to
show succinct okay tomorrows and
yield silver seeds that subsequently
grewed more of them, twice as nice
roasted with lemon thyme and garlic
and more obscure, wild alliums, the
tomorrows, blitzed to a silky soup
for poor camping in the graveyard
under the shade of the willow when
the graveyard had no dead in it yet,
none of the interred being dead,
simply the poor, sharing the soup and
waiting to basically fill the graveyard
up with themselves. The last would

bury the second to last then clamber
on top and sort of draw up the soil
duvet over themselves, starting at the
boots and eventually into the mouth,
the eyes and the ears packed to never
again hear dinner called clear and
mellifluous on the still air from the
beautiful houses beside the graveyard
that were made of imported stone.
There wasn't a graveyard before that
there was just a funny feeling. We did
all we could, I suppose. We gripped
them in our um prayers. We charged
small glasses with a nondescript froth
and raised them to them. We planted
a series of pear trees somewhere,
espaliered like Jesus was, south-
facing in a walled garden crowded
with wild roses in tea-stained, nuptial
ivory, gaoled. Monastic silence, save
for a distant peal and a hot cricket
concert; the gorgeous flat spuff and
tiny metallic report when folding soft
metal caps off of thin glass bottles of
scrumptious, souring perry Hannah
made from the memorial fruit.

Conversations were had between
suppressed belches and quick dogtrot
behind a big bay for hot long release.
So the frying pan sizzle of piss on
sun-dried forage would stir our
appetite for whole sardines, wazzed
with a little lime, skilletted almond
whittles, and more perry for a bonus
voof. We'd in fact eat adult sardines
and we'd dronk a brilliant pale amber
perry Hannah made from pears in
an enchanted walled garden choked
with an astonishing amount of wild
roses in off-white, somewhere easterly
& old. A miraculous hold-out owned
by a family of big evil spiders who
bound the mouldering brickwork as
the strangler's driving gloves they
were like classic masonry wounds
with polished black knees and The
Shakes, debossed in an whole life
of night and the town's gone eyes
gathered in hand-tied bouquets of
cueballs and very rich
desserts.

Lots of unseen movement on the wall
at nighttime. Sounds like the wet pop
of a bakelite mandible or a porcelain
Newton's Cradle coming to rest. The
sounds of nature
were reminiscent; everything
sounded,
to the pit of your stomach. Horrors
fairly trod the undergrowth audibly,
scorned milk in the churn, froze
grapes, turned fruit, ate kiddies, split
mirrors. In the mornings maybe a
dark wet scalp or an undone pink
blouse snagged on pointy teeth.

Perry and sardines used to be taken
beside a heavily spidered wall abutted
by tracts of barren zilch. Barren zilch
were silted and jewelled in the gullies
with a gravel of pink cochineal husks.
Edible looking fish squirmed out their
last, pouted we thought auguries?
and meanwhile their eyes'd clouded,
as with the hot skillet on the fire,
surrounded by its juices, some butter
and oil bubbling. Hissing noised as

the fish's skin got rusted panoply.
Where we'd slashed at it with a long
knife we could make out pale food
peeking through. Wounds would
widen with heat in time and in a field,
in a ditch, we'd cringe beside that
dying fish. Writhing very desperate,
presumably not wanting to die it was
looking at the sky. I put my ear to its
strange mouth to listen to what it had
to say but

it said nothing. Not that there was no
sound at all coming out of its mouth
but that it didn't say

a thing. Whatever it had inside of it
went unsaid

forever.

A gloom descended for a bit and we
just stared at the big
cobalt lobsters
pick
ponderous

paths while um opaline dragonflies
darted above, ideally. We ate all the
animals in any old order, without
cooking them and then we looked at
each other.

Years before, vernal mauve wisteria
affected a kind of peaceable pink
witchery. Visibly stooped under the
weight of a whole host of kittens who
were in quite some pain, it turned out.
We used to stand up very slowly from
the table and
go outside and reach up on our tiptoes
and hand feed the poorly kittens
maybe a casserole and a little or a whit
of some really lovely peach cobbler
and a lovely heavy cream. Then them
then, plucked purring from their
cower and suddenly they needed to
be donated to a ravenous army who
arrived in a cloud of bone-coloured
dust and
cries. The fire shrank from their
yellow eyes and last sighted fun
snuffed out by mud and shit and the

inhuman, red eructations of war.
The soldiers would come forward
in half-remembered formations and
pick up a kitten and eat it, somehow.
Hannah just couldn't. The soldiers
took little or no pleasure at all and
the kittens didn't suffer much. We
understood it for what it was it was
necessary. Blank. Whatever baby
birthday glitter whizz and fairy-cake
sponge had before got dashed against
Brick's edge with all the pliant dead,
upturned gone face. Whatever spark
and zany fizziness husked. Drowned
in a real vomit. If there were any
carefree lush in there to begin with it
had long ago turned a grey Weetabix
cement. Couple of weeks of them and
they left on their knees.

In the autumn we just about managed
birthed a pair of cartoon vultures,
blackest gloss and a harsh eider made
for a awful throbbing exit. They
remain unnamed throughout they
were a bit like animated lab pups? rent

snatch and found a shocking pigswill.
This was it. We'd painted everything
a sable butchery, the walls a pounding
cerise. Prosthetic, mulk and
regurgitated seabird root portioned
on twin cedar spoons in the shape of
our saviour's forearms, stigmatic little
wooden palms upturned. Inside of the
bloody dint in the palms where the
nail would've come and gone maybe
you'd've put a single blueberry or a
slowly levelling tump of molasses.
For our babies we'd mash a few twill
russets with a lot of mum's accidental
yoghurt. An exclusive manuka
drooled in close up from an perfect
comb. Manuka was um meant to
have antibacterial properties and
be synergistic with certain topical
antibiotics squenched from a battered
blue tube but whatever, whenever
we gave benediction to the kids
they bawled for conciliatory meats.
Everyone in hell'd shunned them
before all this and so the shining red
claw had delivered them an womb,

to us but they ate their way out of the
world inside of a bad night. Sundays
we'd more nettles and garner purslane
and tinkling gun blanks, spent and
stirred into a simple warm pomace of
pumpkin, leeks, onion and wild garlic
from a private holt south of the bog.
Weak grey babies did very much like
soup to be slightly hot a little bit more
than the moribund mother's wrung
dud breath. She'd lasted longer than
anyone had had any right to, clutching
at her past with her whiskey'd breath
and dulled horse brasses.

Hannah cradling a woman's head.
The woman feels hot, sick. Hannah
patiently spooning a desultory pink
purée into the woman's pleated little
mouth. Hannah parching apples in
a tin bath in the quad, preparing for
winter. Hannah splitting logs in the
snow and breaking down furniture
and burning it all in the dark in order
to see. The woman doubling over
and heaving nothing into a black

74

plastic crucible and it's hard to watch.
Hannah literally carries everyone.
A wolf sighted on the horizon. A
wolf silhouetted in the twilight. The
woman carries the pestilence and dies
alone.

Mother died far too early and
other people and animals also died
conspicuously early for our liking.
Countless billions, even. Each death
differed from each one other tho there
were undeniable similarities in the
end.

If we'd been allowed to we'd've topped
things off with a preposterous amount
of powdered sugar. Once, we used
to laboriously spaff no small amount
of charmless arm meat down okay
blue tubes, at work. We could turn a
lush flounce and contort tight white
demon pecs, warp-face slicked with
a cool gallon of balked grease. We'd
pour the lot into our glorious laps to
hopefully catch someone's discerning

eye. Some hazy memory of a once
taut dad lap scotched with forsaken
use, maybe. In all seriousness. We
oversaw great tuns of steaming blue
stain. The job involved a rhythmic
over-squat, so that whatever cringing
bit of pork filed against no lining
to a grim red peel, flapped then
clammed. Work meant scouring milt
off Sir's fly. A sorrel cursive, taut
lap. Everything was radically pre-
distressed by some nameless paysan,
a menial horror-graft elsewhere. We
watched as a woman's native sweat
percolated aluminium emulsion
to bloom ivory, slimed ruination,
the pits. Aged Global Hypercolor
resumed belief, but in what?
We imagined a cabal of ad execs
dry-humping in the dark? Ragging
on one another to weft some meagre
measure of I think rayon or ham. Our
superiors would double over, not at
all racked with a nameless delight,
then they'd thump a nice fat shiner
across our ingenuous faces. Indigo

nebulas and semi-preciousness,
uncut. We were riveted. Then we'd
pose naked and they'd envision our
wretched ambition, withering. We'd
lard our hair with some of that tepid
black gook; give it back something of
the mineshaft, the coalface. Or like
a wet pall of her thorts about puffed
affluence with hurled shade. Slogans,
gracious ribcage, opened, glance, you,
help.

Around five we'd assemble more
sandwiches. A naturally occurring
blue margarine, that time, time boiled
ox tongue and white sauce and sweet
romaine and the top bit margarined
too. We really relaxed with these
sandwiches and it was simple, in the
grove. A flat brand of relaxation,
like a normal glove put together
with the other glove that went with
it originally, normally. We'd laugh a
little, haha. I mean, how simple it just
suddenly was to feel basically okay?
when we were together and eating

sandwiches that we liked and
just how absurd, etcetera. We
addressed each other in the face,
smiling but now that the sandwiches
had gone they had been eaten using
the same face but in a different
mode. The mode of eating. Our
teeth were by this point just munted
bullrush nubs. We'd not be eating
the sandwiches anymore but instead
tracking pain in another's mouth.
Sometimes pain cut a pink ceramic
blade, chicken things from Findus.
Sometimes a trashy pink rubber toy,
spuffing a little in the oil, spluttering
impediment, *outrage* – cooking flames
shot thru with lurid chemical um
colours. Then buffing the ashes into
dad's personal latrine and the water
would went elderly just like him did
he was like a old Berocca adamant
in stout. He'd bloody well bark at a
golden sword if he'd only had one.
Saturdays spent making a delicate
piccalilli to go with some boiled
sausages a passing kindly rich sort

parsimoniously unfurled from her
clutch on to the porch a week prior.
She was on her way to a kind of
heaven it looked like, judging by Her
Hems and Her anaemic skin shone.

Cauliflower florets, softening red
onions from a blue plastic crate, sea
salt, mustard oil, mustard seeds,
cumin, turmeric, nutmeg, white
wine vinegar, sugar, a small group of
purpling garlic cloves, oregano, bay,
chilli if we had had it. Cauliflowers
were really great. Brained, crook
broccoli; a damp mummified corpse
of trees was tasty as. Sometimes
a chargrilled stroke victim, other
times a toddler's prop. A slowed
cheddar bog inuring insipidity but
it was everyone's absolute favourite
and it was simple for us to make. We
encouraged everyone to try making
it it was stupidly easy to make. And
though necessity was the mother of
invention, we ate an easy, sluggish
cauliflower cheese clag for a good few

years in the middle, when everything
was especially difficult, financially
and so on. Poverty meant spongiform
and otherwise compressed veg. —
Compressed as in coal or crude.
Megafauna and prehistoric fronds
and sacrificed offsprung mashed
by millennia's shining plate mitt,
Armoured God.
We had to drink the starless fluid that
would gurgle from a wound in a rock
above the tree-line. Black and umber,
a profound nout.

Weekends scouring furrowed mud
brows near just over there, in a
persistent drencher, slouched in
shallow graves where a company
of potatoes' eyes shot grey burgeon
thru ruddy mud gum, so gored or
put out with an iron fork. We would
pause there, on a squat scarp between
peasant plots, naked and rain-slick,
nothing else for it, each of us waylaid
by loads of blind potatoes in thin wet
white pillowcases. We'd survey a dim

prospect
all about and feel that raw and
irresolvable concretion of weakness
quease a little down there in our
empty tums, you know? Still — we'd
remember while foundering down
the bank — when chipped and fried
and shuffled fresh into tabloid passels
with a plentiful Sarson's piddle and an
extravagance of table salt. Everyone
really liked chips with plenty frosty
copas.
A nicely going head on a bright
wallop.
Chips were hot and golden and
flashing with fat, all crisped tips and
scalding lint cores. Big ones clunged
together, spent warm dongers between
working forefingers. Vinegar bloated.
Splintery little shivs that rasped the
palate. Perfectly direct batons an even
tan, exhaled piping vinegar vape to
rouse a prickle of sweat to runnel the
caked coal dust. Chillered, hoppy
lager spumed the glorious chip pulp
down everyone's then slake gullets.

Hot & cold, fizz & flat, earthy pap.
Everyone who worked incredibly
hard at their job enjoyed chips. The
people, a giggly chip pleasure over
the course of one lunchtime quite
despite or because of the end of the
chips' gleeful trespass, then back to
work. Recklessly stored energy soon
enough squandered on an impossible
job that totally broke you.

In the cold, disentangling sundered
fingers from a witch-hazel thicket
outside the butcher's. Gratitude
expressed carefully, in drummed
morse ordnance of rejected carrion,
some leagues hence.
We arrived about 11pm, the night
before winter solstice.

We were bound in blue tarp and torn
rubble bags and glossy supplements
against the gale and inside of an
cave this heaving black spangled
coverlet of juiceless horseflies sucked
and blewed enzymic icing over an

indiscernible but goodly commons
pile. An microtonal norro pitch shoft
inside the flies' paper drone like
allotment shortwave. Shooed with a
flourish of the flaming torch then we
unhesitating um lay into it, uncertain
of really how to prep carrion other
than with a tenderising kicking. A
limestone sand, then, steeped with off-
brown blood wrung in the kicking.
A bristle of froze grass shew at the
mouth, portending Christ or sprung
from a Zion. Schmaltz fairly seeped
from the pallid underneath, where
soft and perishable wobbled when we
rolled it over stuck over with natural
floor stuff. A big spoon gouged simple
dupe on a slice of sour pumpernickel,
just slipped under a medium grill.
Served with sweet tears bangles of
uncooked white onion to basically just
gently contest the enervated fat that'd
be in the mouth, that's all. Hanks
from the top pared afters bobbed in
a hot brodo thicker with arrowroot
meant a raging fever.

Christmas figments hung
in the air.
We hauled all the meat outside in
the morning and dumped it among
the lightly tortured roots of a beech
tree and got sensible of the divine
via sweet box dark berries and dark
glossy leaves, winter aconite and
hellebores sissyed the way back,
astonishingly. Red berries to the East,
then, mealy new snow, dotted with
the hacked consumption, pulmonary
as the seasons then were. Rattling
inhalation of our final planet was, past
its autumn, winter cooling morsels
of hot angel skeletons between the
earth's sequoial molars, pulling
cooling atmospheres over the bones,
plainted on pleather tongue tract,
in the moist dark and the reek of
mephitic sod. Wood molars ill champ,
then, as-if on a grilled prawn's outer
only
it was angel scrag, like Murano spun
sugar acquired sunlight. We hung
a mute squall on a sett horizon and

seven-foot copper angels hurtled
through the pearl cloudburst to the
sea, dead. Exhaled summers lapped
yellow beaches paced by small taupe
crabs and the first adorable humans
someplace else.

Most of the time what we had was this
pleural self-supper. Brought up from
inside ourselves like a love
a sort of cud, chewed with some
brown leaves from the driveway and
horrible, salt rained retch spazzed,
swallowed again and again an till
heaved up one of the more vital
purple organs and you had to go to
the clinic then and have it removed.
Autocannibalism seemed more
virtuous and somehow easier, also,
especially when given the choice
between a really personable infant or
one of your own limbs.
They'd told pork was
similar to human flesh but it wasn't at
all. There was a big utensil a bit like
Hannah's secateurs but for human

limbs instead of leylandii. It took
three strong operators to then lower
the top acute bit through a trussed
thigh then ratchet it to reset, ready for
another one. You used to have to wait
a while between chopping but that
was out of a respect that we couldn't
really afford no not for long anyways.
Also quite quickly everything was
done by computer, so. So instead
we'd lavish our time on a sexual whit
and linger deep felt hatred for all
kinds of authority Also knowledge
acquisition, abstract sensations of
inherited specialness.
From the sick bed, beneath a lively
quilt, Fridays a penitent wild rice
pilaf, a steamed branzino, literally
no seasoning, fondling and kissing
this way and that and all the while
thin unperfumed steam rose from
pilaf and fish together, brought in on
the yellow tray, smuggled beneath
the covers to eat. Hannah'd boarded
up the windows for good. We hid
our love right up inside ourselves,

afraid of what others might've done
if they'd've clocked it. Hence all
the penetrations and the listening
in on things from outside of our
own heads and looking everyplace
but mirrors. Pressing up the hard
crumbs and crystals with our wetted
fingers. Hoovered up multi-coloured
powders, other's sighed junk smoke
as they fall back, a little fucking bad
baff. We ingested things from the
outside when we could and we took
in strangers also into our bodies. We
practiced a profane grace, open to
both the switch and the caress, eyes
fastened & mouths agape to accept
a loaded dessertspoon or, like, a
whining dental wand.
We repudiated choice we used to tilt
our necks for vampires.
We used to tilt our necks and coyly
just tuck our bangs behind A ear
and sway there like marionettes, that
inviting sugared pout playing on our
lips, warm meated breath shallow and
anticipatory.

We ate fishfingers from a silver
platter, once.

A boy with a long thin head and these
faint eyes who has since really sadly
passed got into bed. He would get into
bed like a wizard he brought with
him all these silvery little animals
he'd named. He had all his own teeth
and he had these lips like a scuttled
dirigible and a pervasive, marshalling
way of kissing with them. He could
open his face like maybe a pink-
carpeted toilet seat and he had an
edible regret we pecked like little
sexy plovers.
Through June people visited us for
sex. We'd an insatiable capacity
to ingest feelings of worthlessness
like so much slack salad. For many
years we'd a venereal proclivity,
gastronomically and emotionally
speaking. Mark put sharp rage in
our mouths, candlelit, with our easy
consent. A rigid lurcher but a smooth
pewtered mellow tang. Ristretto

chasers, limoncello cloy. He ate us
prodigiously and us him, too, he was
oiled coasted a clove rub, numbed
on top and it was so-so. We were, I
think, to one another, glazed hams
repast in a hot stint, pocked with
squeaking pickled eyeballs.

Simple, plain cod cheeks on whatever
heel of bread you have to hand it
doesn't matter at all. Maybe a little
butter that's all a little sriracha which
is just a type of hot-sauce. Grim
regulars would without fail shot out
premature gun of sputter when we
slid the plates under their noses.
Cod cheek on approx. stottie fumed
then we got you out of your bag and
threw you at the room. We'd also
make sandwiches for the kids and
any persons who didn't really eat
complicated stuff maybe just moved
the bits around the plate or had a
notably disordered way with eating.
We would cater.

Plowing in March and April. Downey little leveret hares drilled on fresh pastures, nibbling petrified, crapping currants, herded by wiry, lunatic parents. We'd watched them from the kitchen window, faced with

our eviction but things seemed to be getting better, we had had to admit it?

Hares were a poor choice of foods because of their really very low fat content not to mention how very beautiful and special they were. We were more or less content to ogle them on leaden mornings, over a porcelain basin, mixing up flour we um had with maybe barley or oats, fava beans, fresh chestnuts, maybe vetches slopped on black trencher bread instead of plates we'd sold the plates and weren't allowed to use any bequeathed porcelain, not to us, of course, sat plumb in the china hutch, ever unused, gilded and wreathed and monogrammed and mocking.

Moistened our bodies, cooled our
bodies over and over. Soups and
potages were improved somewhat
thickened with hare's blood we
brutally snared and pied and bled
dead to the last hare. We wore dyed
hare caps and thought hare face were
felicitous when flattened and pinned
to a lapel.

Gruel, milk soups? We imagined we
fucking deserved to be this low.

We knew proportionality when

we were forced to ingest it with a tube
probity felt as an over-lubed tube
muscled down the nasogastric flue.
An watery graviesed awoitsed. So
gavaged we'd try sell our extorted
intimate livers to a dedicated body
that was wholly just, tight-fisted he
wanted to eat them, understandably,
smoked over a cherry-wood fire while

we watched, sweating small change
and pearl onions inside tight fists,
eyes dewed for kaleidoscopic sweet
flame. Put on toast it looked like
maybe a busted gorgon.

Previously, we made what we liked to
call ragout which main's ingredient
was yet a brayed nettle bread of
butcher's paper we got free. Weeds,

filth, sawdust we got free, nettles.
Straw for nuncheon, rank wine sop
cupped in puffy nettle-stang hands.

We used to have very very powerful
wind pretty much all the time. It was
very very funny but also distressing
in its constancy its overwhelming
heckle we could scarcely hold a
conversation that wasn't punctuated
with histrionic blasts and piffle from
one or other flapping bumhole.
We aren't sick we're miserable,
Hannah would say.

If you want to make a flat meat cake,
take meat from the belly and take
marrow, says Hannah. And see to it
that it is boiled really well and chop it

up small. And grate half as much
cheese add it to it, mix it with eggs so
that it thickens, season with pepper,
and put it on a thin dough you have.
And put it into the oven and let it
bake. Serve it hot if you can. Voilà,
a flat meat cake. If you really want
mig-raust with almond milk, do it
this way first roast hens. Then take
stock made from other hens and make
stock with the insides of the hens plus
salted pork; and then take blanched
almonds and make milk with the
stock. And take the livers and pound
them well and mix them with the
milk I said. And make this boil with
pepper, ginger, cloves, cinnamon,
and add a sour ingredient of your
choosing and white sugar. And boil
all this until you know for sure it's
cooked then serve it in bowls together

with hens and if you wish, serve the
hens on platters. If you want to make
Golden Apples and other things take
raw pork and grind it very small with
the grinder. And mix it with strong
powder, saffron, salt, currants. Roll it
into balls and wet it well in egg white
and cook it in boiling water. Take
them out and put them on a spit. Roast
them well. Take ground parsley and
press together with eggs and plenty
of flour and let the paste flow from
over the spit. And if you wish, take
saffron instead of parsley and serve
it forth. Cut up your hens fry them
with pork fat and with onions; and
while they are frying add a little
water so that they cook nicely. And
stir them often with a large spoon.
Add spices, saffron and verjuice and
boil. And for each hen take the four
yolks and mix them with verjuice
and boil this separately. And beat
everything together in the pan and
boil everything with the pieces of
hen. And when it boils remove it and

eat it. Take mutton, veal or pork and chop it up all small then boil hens and quarter it. And the other meat must be cooked before being chopped up. And then get powder and sprinkle it on the meat sensibly and fry your meat in grease. And then get those open pastry shells and shape them with crenelations; they should be of a sturdy dough so you can hold the meat. If you want you can mix pine-nut paste and currants among the meat? And with granulated sugar on top into each pasty put three or four hens quarters in which to plant the banners and glaze them with moistened saffron to make them better. And when the pies are filled with the meat the meat on top should be glazed with a little spew of beat egg, yolks and whites, so this meat will hold together solid enough to stick the banners in to it. And you should have gold-leaf or silver-leaf to glaze the pies before setting the banners in them.

        Hannah copies this out for
us and
she

leaves in the dead of night and where
are we we carnt understand it not
at all. Hannah signs off, then her
signature and then what looks like a
little x, a little kiss, for us.

Spring came and went, weft dredged
green godweaves of gutweed found
drowned emissaries off the dock with
a piece of plastic piping, a length of
blue string and a wire coat hanger into
a pink moulded plastic castle bucket.
We'd get some adults to help clean
it thoroughly not in the tod brine
but in tin baths of hard water tap. In
went lots of children, all about their
badly skinned knees, loosely applied
dressings, elbow scabs, gelled snot,
the very turdy fun. Then deep fried
scabs of umami gutweed very easily
crumbled between the fingers over a
midweek tagliatelle even deemed an

easy win for mum the working mum,
is blasted by her temp work, too. A
lasagne from the shops it had that
horse's pinto rendered in bechamel
and grill acne. An indescribable
taste it was from the basic range.
Unrecognisable lasagne basically a
puddle angrily trying to right itself.

We would burned our tongues on
lasagnes.
We consoled our tongues with cold
semi-skimmed.
The horse's face surfaced, then, like
homesickness inside of our dreams
that very night. An heavy wet cake;
the flames of a fire; a limping white
tom, forecourt. A fantastical world
map. It had a juicy role in a baffling
story related by a small
other evil woman at the bar who,
drunk, took our bets. Her herding to
her static caravan her son's profile in
the net-curtained nicotine perspex,
she says, and its the shadow of the
old horse on a man, et velvet muzzle

twotched curtain moist puff murked
his splintered hoof scratched A
welcome. Her hands gestured ushered
to us, her charges, inside her home
for what looked like her own game
but turned into her saddest ballad, her
son, served, once, and her husband
apparently left, citing her and her
hands turned to mending but for one
she just couldn't and he'd cursed her
soldiered son her only son, her son
come back changed, by war, so gone,
we'd've said, only herd welcomed
extended, her hands her son
shouldered burdensed, clonking guns
and big chains, red fuel tanks, her
son, then, septic in bits, basically, her
son this um shrieking horse-headed
son her son'd dronk with nope, no
mirrors just yellowed, fragile plaque
hooves kept rigid in soldered boots'd
& not delicate white gloves, though,
for snooker but hoofed, her son'd
cooked up this utterly startling
shortcrust poke with local songbirds
in it and leeks, she was so proud but

he'd still couldn't smiled or look
anything like an son her son and
maybe'd it'd wasn't him at all whoat
come back from the war just an old
terrified horse got up to look like her
son her son parodied by the enemy a
final hurt. She wished her son super
well and truly put him down with our
help and put her gun into his head.

We'd a breakfast and later we
refinanced the hovel in which curved
posh comed
enviably dry, dronk were enough to
burn only one meagre throat they
didn't pay enough and we lost out an
vast amount.

By winter it was just the one, put on a
cheap slice of white under really a lot
of Stork marg stodge put and a lone
Kraft slice that's all with a generous
spoonful of impish brown own-brand.
Cold grey beef panels squibbed the
excess cloyed, tough love waylaid. In
a wicker bath chair, maybe. Dot dijon,

then. A couple crisp alien wingcases
of the venal gem in lawn green only
one firm orange tomato sliced thick,
latitudinally. Maldon, then, and one
or two twists of black pepper that's
all. Then simply more of the same
bread just put on the top simple as
that like a simple drawing of a hat and
malt vinegar. We'd do lots of these in
cling and place them in the road in
runoff in winter.

For four long years we squatted on
minus-twelve, the live-work rut of
a fifty-storey KST, the weight and
warmth was sufficient to fuck us to
curved trilobite dimensions, fossilised
in a basement caramel. Over the
warped dining table terrible slugs
we pawed a lot of worms with hands
or it could've been our inaccurate
feet it didn't matter it was mercifully
very dark. The depth and warmth
were sufficient to found the live-
work bakery it was the right kind
of atmosphere and just a great vibe

in there for proving pregnant loam
loaves wired with pink worms and
whiskery root nibs that eased through
the walls forever, bunting innards
from an ceiling. The floor was tiled
with a lot of iron hexes you could
get, you could badly fry or sear a
careless foot on them so we perforce
got good at a very funny looking
totter abroad thin paths of thermal
black mud between the hexes, herding
the tummied doughs till such time as
when then thin dermal crust formed
and worms and sour fungal taps
perished, stopped moving offensively.
It was a genital sauna down there and
we could maybe sell them to really
hopeless people in the basement
with us and then beneath that in
their basement and so on. Anyone
higher up than minus-two had at
least some access to hot milt and suds,
scum, bastards dined out on steeped
hand water stromed off of reeking
waxed Barbours, upstairs. Barbours
bequeathed for a succession of

cunts who'd pocket satsumas, rough oatcakes, Fox's. Snacks not food, so replete they were and somehow they always stank of cold diesel.

Remember Hannah would scramble up thru the tiers? Between jutting bodies, a few parts the right temperature, attempted bartering our bread as she went, getting medicines and spices and some ethyl in part exchange at a market on minus-six right where the tower's foundations visibly founded and people even had toilets and language and basically lives. Joint ointments and something for the eyes: peppercorns and the wondrous dulling ethyl, we'd've shot in cedar shooters to shock a spine or skull into rattling action. Our skin was lost to the dark and the tiny lech of constant worm touch. My premium snot were a brown condiment glass bottle thread coagulate? An issue, really, and we'd secrete also oils with a high smoke-point from our skins.

We thought that maybe we could also
sell these oils to someone but no one
wanted
it at all and Hannah could usually
be counted on to shift just about
anything. Hannah'd head for the
surface. It wasn't your gormless
brown or black like now or in really
any way dark as it is nowadays but
rather striped A alien Acquafresh
jingo, only alimentarily let, dulled
argil for shite through countless
generations begot absolutely no eyes
in the end.

Eyes were terminally deputised by
tight little dots over years. Tight
holes. Gaps with red nerves coming
out
a bit. New punctuation was
unreadable as it was it was our eyes
and we knew nothing of how it all
worked though admittedly we'd um
pack the dirt in there in the sockets
with a care that might've convinced
we'd did.

Oils, besides, were abundant at
least when it was like this like it
was misgiven just past porches via
surrendered pores. Dying people lost
a lot of their oils in the end. They
were exceptionally hard to replace
and their bodies really needed them,
sadly. Nearly everybody spent lots of
time trying to sell their own leaking
oils, not knowing how in the hell to
replace them and being bewilderingly
poor. Oftentimes a person died
surrounded by browning plastic
bottles of their own characteristic oil,
dismally peddled at a dark junction
somewhere several miles from their
birth. Some were people we knew.
I think maybe someone or some
official body collected those remains
and did something with them and
the bottled oils that was respectful,
sentimentality covering for, Jesus,
just this profound hunger that felt like
a brother conjoined inside of you.
Sometimes A pelt and A being, teeth
and B. 2 Eyes cabled together,

A red biro scrawled over & hard-boil
clacker if you listened but also
compelled a close gobble of intra
crimson, blasted starve. We'd grapple
our guts as the thin gut-wall bivouacs,
terrified of the process surely
transpiring within. Yoked space set
firm, convicted brothers in each of us,
lifers and it hurting like anything.

There was sometimes a recollection
of tunnels that were so warm and so
moist and so heavy with sulphuric
slip you could have proven a niche
dough there and some people actually
used to do that. Bracketing finally a
bland sandwich meat but that's okay.
Best employed in a cinch like that.
Like a dinghy and about as flavourful.
Barely a boat low in the brew /
a sandwich meat crew.
There was corned crew liveried in
Poupon cords and kalamata galoshes
and sered. Cambered in the drink.
Squibbed old
daft songs from a Alba decay filed

steel bars and smashed great red
ceramic hornfuls on black rocks,
swallowed by the space, the seabirds'
yelp and a crashed scum come spewed
big crumb mouthfuls, perhaps a beer
reinvigorating olde coral rims, swoll
to meet teeth that'd forced
the cheeks swoll up in the first place
by biting them because they, the teeth,
maybe mistook some eminence of
cheek for maybe the hake or some
game in Guinness inside the queer
dugout of your mouth. Drowning
became choking, then dry.

There used to be innumerable
chock of paled plastics dammed the
shoreline. A torpid midriff fleshed out
on and on.Rolling hills looked like
maybe ha toffee paper and costumier
schmuck prodded by the midday sun
and were, basically, but we didn't get
it really this was just a lot of death sat
there part-bridging continents and
smelling of a stranded rock-pool or
Hannah's abalone parts.

There were toilets but they were
filled up with our precursors' poorly
contents. Leather kidney bean chaff,
plastic shrimp armour and panning
undigested sweetcorn glant in the
light of a shared match's guttering

little flame.
We usually went at home where
at least the pooing were familial,
familiar. There was a documented
dissonance between the nigh-nothing
we put in and the copious, unfurling
horrors we put out in the corner near
the breakfast table. When the sun
finally came up it found several glad
fried eggs of some reality and a rack
of triangular white toast and an pot of
bath coffee and orange juice with bits
in. Maybe a whistling kettle, steam
clothed light, a gyre of black shit in
the corner right up to the ceiling. We
wanted for nothing we didn't even
have that. Hannah tried but there was
nothing nor for it.

We wanted for maybe a sugared
nothing
and in short order we did not survive.

Years of this kitchen scene.
Everything spoiled and moreover
time, except for the black shit which
the other things came to resemble
before everything, indistinguishable,
was summarily buried under a big
subsidence of earth.

After dinner in Hamburg in an
October we only had one pink
toilet with a pink corded surround
harbouring you can guess microbial
riot and another oval one on the
lid for touching, the motions and
satisfaction ebbed with each urgent
knocking at the door. We'd read
fun books and magazines from a
warped pile by the u-bend, glossy
newspaper supplements embarrassed
by an aerosol of piss to measle a
Cover Someone from years before.
Cookery books' confused stains from

before and after, grease and caress,
whichever hand didn't wipe or glued
pages with a failing dough concretised
like the lanes of brown that poorly
sketched the bowl and no velocity of
wee at all were sufficient to dislodge
and the brush's head also drowned
in a bog scat too in brown poo, like
how the cooker's hood was caked in
animal fat and the smut from the oil,
soot, dusts. One night we towed a
teaspoon through it and saw the stuff
satisfyingly corkscrew like a butter
ad that was popular. We would do this
a number of times and then line the
corkscrewed ort up
on the hood of the cooker to slowly
return to a coat. Then
we'd go outside for some air and peace
and have a cigarette and a drink, my
god.

Summer.

Words' nutritional nothing despite
the quality of the writing lyric meant
fuck all to our carping tummies,
and the gripping epic we'd read only
razed colons, tunnelling turded
stanzas enjambed oesophaguses
very much bust up our already
bullied pancreases so pancreatitis
sprant a pink and painful flue and
cupping with a bad type of diabetes
laid waste to our wild meadowed
guts and all but shredded the secret
glades – the hearts of love, silvered
inedible filo – a distended steel
barrel shacked ferments and arrived
all of a sudden with a live cultural
ethos turned horribly easily into
incontrovertible morality. As a
consequence everyone turned into
vampires. But a world chock with
vampires and no humans meant
for dowdy reality of vampirism.
Surgical, expensively administered
cannibalism. Big pharma shodding
jugged plasma. They, the vampires,
would sup an arterial rot in black

cowls on moors in mist. Used to
be that oceans of blood turned a
terrifying black and poisonous to
mug the species which ceased, had
had enough and everything turned
away from the sun which, entirely
unregarded by god or leaf, turned to
a red skull howled with a high soot
and then there was just this chasmic
sigh hooed over the spent earth.
In the outdoor swimming pools:
vampires. At the busted gates of hell:
vampires. Parliament: unbroken
vampires. High Heaven: tweaking
innumerable vampires vermillion
droppings smeared about and those
dragged vampire glands across the
very walls of heaven? Liverish all,
forever-prison, abiding and feral and
so, so dead. Everyday was forever,
was a complete non-starter, same as
every other till One day there came
this perfect silence, this perfect noise,
each eye spitting a glue at one another
really very close to one another. An
eternal rasp lapped incorrectly at

nothing. Back then eternity clawed at
Mist on Dirt and guzzled insatiable,
eventually getting round to classic
fossils, statues, red bus haunches torn
from the chassis. Altogether, weeks
were brought low and supernaturally
cretinous, condemned us. Mirrors
emptied at us, recasting only opaque
grim light for years till the foil rent.
Ill wind, frankly, gutted songbirds
mid-flight in a so-called spring, so
that even the history of death felt
much worse with gutted songbirds
smirched flyblown pottages. We
failed to escape and so for many
years were forced to feed on Scour
Vermin else turn likewise. Rat crack
painted with putty-coloured cuckoo
spit straight out the tube, advanced
contents served over a rot thatch
paffed beside fresh-cull rammed
wee curds or what we would called
bread sauce. Humans' blood steeped
a solitary wheat-sheaf when all wheat
went away. A shave meant a meal of
urine-soured stubble. Glimmers like

that. Chocolate coins seemed doubly
cryptic with the collapse of the
banks and the rise of the vampires.
Vampires skulked in haunted banks
and twiddled those little yellow nets
of chocolate coins in their claws,
quizzically, making that horrid,
ubiquitous ticking sound. Then
they'd snick the yellow mesh and just
let the chocolate coins fall onto the
dirt and grind the chocolate coins into
the dirt with their ornately spurred
boot-heels. Then they'd dart off,
tinkling. On the very last day they
took a dairy cow's mother cake and
forced it through the chainlink fence
with a stolen malacca, unsmiling. The
bits landed in some intricate white
dirt. If eked out, dirt-crust placenta
meant another week and they fucking
knew it. Tossed about in a Panda
Coke or something and bolted with
a searing paste of raw, electroplated
catholic garlic, flat.
The vampires were in the air!,
howling and shitting and whirling

about in the scorched sky like diabolic
kites. Months dragged and did for
us and we succumbed, falled ripped
sullied and blethering on our knees
and begging so

we pierced the crust with our hot new
really long cute cuspids and drained
the very molten core, triggering the
cataclysm and palled the spent earth
with a billion black wings. The new
moon was there and there were a new
there herald pipe spring.

Acknowledgements

'Old Food' started life as an exhibition, originally for
the Martin-Gropius-Bau in Berlin, and subsequently
 at Cabinet Gallery, London; Kunsthaus Bregenz; K21
in Düsseldorf, and the Venice Biennale. It consisted
of eight and then nine videos; anywhere between eight
hundred and a few thousand costumes sourced from opera
houses and theatres; and a series of enigmatic wall texts
written by Contemporary Art Writing Daily and laser-
etched onto locally-sourced garbage wood. This text, 'Old
Food', was written in blurts throughout, I suppose, only
really reaching a palpable form in early 2019 after infinite
processes of impoverishment. I've read chunks of it to
audiences at Gavin Brown's Enterprise in New York; the
Royal College of Art, London; Kunsthaus Bregenz; my
students at Det Kongelige Danske Kunstakademi, and as
part of a reading organised by Steven Zultanski — both in
Copenhagen. There is also a pretty hysterical recording
for Cold Protein of the first part, entitled 'Flat Meat Cake'
and to be listened to on the toilet in the McDonalds in
Leicester Square, London. 'Old Food' became 'Olde Food'
at Cabinet and then, to ram home the chalk pen pub sign,
'Ye Olde Food' in Düsseldorf.

Thank you Simon Thompson, Adam Thirlwell, Steven
Zultanski, Joe Luna, Martin McGeown, Dan Fox, Tom
Brewer, Mike Sperlinger, Sonya Merutka, Helen Marten,
Contemporary Art Writing Daily, Martin Herbert, Pablo
Larios, Thomas Oberender, Lisa Marei-Schmidt, Kathy
Noble, Beatrice Hilke, Susanne Gaensheimer, Thomas
Trommer, Ralph Rogoff. Thanks to my mother and my
brother and my dead dad. Thank you dearest Sally-Ginger
and darling Hollis Pinky.

Fitzcarraldo Editions
8-12 Creekside
London, SE8 3DX
United Kingdom

ISBN 978-1-910695-93-7

Design by Ray O'Meara
Typeset in Fitzcarraldo
Printed and bound by TJ International

fitzcarraldoeditions.com

Fitzcarraldo Editions